This book belongs to

_____

_____

For Honor and Leon
G.G.

For Ann and her big heart
R.A.

This edition published by Parragon Inc in 2013

Parragon Inc.
440 Park Avenue South, 13th Floor
New York, NY 10016
www.parragon.com

Published by arrangement with Gullane Children's Books
185 Fleet Street, London, EC4A 2HS

Text © Greg Gormley 2013
Illustrations © Roberta Angaramo 2013

ISBN 978-1-4723-2429-0
Printed in China

Pick Me!

Greg Gormley • Roberta Angaramo

Bath • New York • Singapore • Hong Kong • Cologne • Delhi
Melbourne • Amsterdam • Johannesburg • Shenzhen

It was visitors' day at the animal shelter
and Dog was determined to get
a very special owner.

There were plenty to choose from:
tall, elegant dukes,
sparkling movie stars in gold dresses,
and powerful presidents.

So when an **ordinary** little girl smiled at Dog,
he stuck his sniffy nose in the air
and turned his back on her.

But as a great and graceful ballet dancer arrived,
Dog did his best to impress her.

He spun on the tips of his pointy paws . . .

and leaped high into the air.

"Pick me!"

said Dog.

But he landed in a muddy
puddle right up to his tummy.
He looked like he was wearing
chocolate pants.

The great and graceful ballet dancer
was not impressed at all.

Then along came a famous entertainer.
Dog bounced up and down on a large ball
while balancing a dessert on the end of his nose.

"Pick me!"

said Dog.

But he slipped
and the creamy dessert flew everywhere.
The famous entertainer walked on.

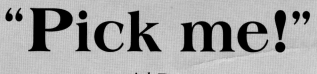

Next, a much admired
conductor appeared.
Dog blew into a slide trombone
while rattling a triangle
with his tail.

"Pick me!"

said Dog.

But the slide trombone
slid in two and Dog's bottom
got stuck in the triangle.

The much admired conductor shook his head.

Finally, a most important artist took a look at Dog.

Dog covered his tail in different colors
then used it like a paintbrush.

"Pick me," said Dog.

But great blobs of paint
spattered everything,
making a terrible mess.

The artist ran away in horror.

Dog felt desperate.
**"No one special
will pick me now,"**
he whimpered.

**"Yes, they will,
don't worry,"**
a voice said . . .

It was the
ordinary little girl.

She got soap and water.
She washed off the mud,
the dessert and the paint.

She slid the trombone
back together, pulled the
triangle off Dog's bottom . . .

then she gave Dog a good brushing.
"Perfect," she said.